Making Plum Jam

John Warren Stewig

ILLUSTRATED BY Kevin O'Malley

HYPERION BOOKS FOR CHILDREN

NEW YORK

To the memory of those real-life aunts,
Alice, Lizzie, and Jane,
who were such an important influence
on my life
—J.W.S.

The car bounces on the rutted gravel road between rows of cornstalks taller than the car's roof. This August, like every year, we're on the way to the farm, where I spend a week with my mother's aunts.

"Now, Jackie, just *think* before you do anything," Mom reminds me. "You know the aunts sometimes do things differently than we do."

I don't say anything about the fact that that's the reason I like coming here. Everything is so different from the way it is at home.

There's Aunt Jane, standing in the clearing in the midst of the grove. She's the oldest and thinnest, and she runs across the grass to our car. "What did you learn in school this year that I should know?" she asks.

There's Aunt Lizzie, the middle aunt, waiting for us on the crooked stoop. "There are seven new kittens in the barn you'll want to look at," she tells me.

I wave to Aunt Alice, who's waiting in her porch rocker. "Come here and give me a big hug!" she demands.

Dad helps me carry my suitcase upstairs, while Mom follows the aunts into the kitchen to help get dinner on the table.

After our arrival, we all sit around the kitchen table, "full up" as usual with fried chicken, mashed potatoes and gravy, fresh-from-the-garden beans, and Aunt Alice's specialty, chokecherry pie. We're all sitting crooked, because the floor tilts. Was it always slanted, or did the house get tired because it's even older than the aunts? The flickering light from the kerosene lamp makes my eyelids droop. "Why don't you have electricity yet, Aunt Jane?" I ask.

"It's just plain stubbornness," my mother answers for her. "All the other farms on the road have electricity by now."

"That's good enough for all the rest, and kerosene is good enough for us," Aunt Alice responds. "You seemed to enjoy trimming the wicks when you were our little girl who came to visit." Mom says that was too long ago to remember.

When she hugs me good-bye, her look tells me to be good.

Next morning when I wake up, sun fingers are stretching across the floor. I like sleeping under the slanted ceiling. I'm wide awake, thinking about visiting the new barn kittens and my friend from last summer, Homer the pig.

When I come down for breakfast, Aunt Alice is stirring pancake batter in a heavy bowl. I look in the frying pan. "Is that . . . ?" I begin, not able to say his name.

"Yes, it's Homer, but it *is* tasty bacon," Aunt Alice says as she spoons rounds of batter onto the griddle and Aunt Lizzie puts a plate of sizzling strips in front of me.

Homer! I push the bacon over to the side of my plate so I won't have to eat him. The aunts can, but I won't.

As we eat, we talk. There's lots of talk with the aunts, as always, though I mostly listen.

Finally we get down to the important talk of planning our day.

Chores always have to be done first, but they're different from the ones at home. I like these better. First, I help Aunt Jane gather the still-warm eggs, slop this year's pig, and water the runner beans, same as last year. But that only takes part of the morning. What shall we do next?

Aunt Alice says, "It's early for jam making, but ours is almost gone." Jam! I've never made jam with the aunts before.

"Can we make jam from chokecherries?" I ask.

"They're already canned up," Aunt Jane replies.

"Raspberries?" I ask.

"They won't be sweet for another month," Aunt Lizzie tells me.

"Well, there's always that plum tree in Farmer Wilson's yard," Aunt Alice says.

"Farmer Wilson?" I ask.

"Bought the old Gilfilan farm," Aunt Alice tells me. "Madge Gilfilan always gave us plums every summer, right up to the year she died." Aunt Alice declares, "Those young bachelor farmers don't know anything about making jam."

After chores, we all climb into the old Ford coupe. "The horse was always more reliable," Aunt Lizzie says every time we get into the car. I'm wedged in the back beside Aunt Lizzie. Aunt Alice lines up the left wheels on the centerline as we turn onto the main road. The few cars that come toward us veer over into the opposite ditch. When she shifts, the car pauses, trying to make up its mind. We go really slowly, so I can see even the dust on the soybean leaves. When my dad drives, the car moves so fast I can hardly see anything.

Aunt Alice noses the car toward the ditch. When we all get out, the car doors' slamming disturbs the quiet. Aunt Lizzie bends down the branches, while Aunt Alice and I pull plums into the splintery basket. "Don't let them fall on the ground," Aunt Alice directs us. "Bruised fruit doesn't make sweet jam."

We've harvested most of the ripest plums when a louder sound crowds out the quiet summer noises. A distant motor is coming closer. A red-faced farmer is barreling down on us, riding a tractor taller than our car, shaking his fist. Farmer Wilson! Aunt Alice said he doesn't make jam, but I guess that doesn't make any difference to him.

Aunt Alice shoos me into the fold-forward seat of the car, like a chicken into a coop. Aunt Lizzie barely squeezes in before Aunt Jane and Aunt Alice slam the doors shut. The farmer can see we're leaving, but he comes toward us, shouting angry words my mother says I cannot use.

Aunt Alice shifts into first gear and hurries down the road at twenty-five miles an hour, faster than she's ever driven before. The farmer chases us, shaking his straw hat. At last we leave him behind in the Minnesota dust. "I don't know what he was so upset about," Aunt Alice declares, as we pull into the road leading to the house.

"It isn't as if he was going to make jam," Aunt Lizzie responds. "It's a waste for those plums to fall to the ground to feed chipmunks and squirrels."

"You can measure out the sugar," Aunt Alice tells me, "while Aunt Jane pits the plums and Aunt Lizzie sterilizes the jars."

"What are *you* going to do?" I ask.

"I'll supervise," Aunt Alice announces. Supervising is what Aunt Alice does best. Soon the kitchen smells of plums bursting their jackets in boiling water. The floor is gritty with sugar underfoot. Watching Lizzie plunge the glass jars, caged in the metal basket, into the huge tub of scalding water to sterilize them is almost as exciting as being chased by an angry farmer, I think. Later, the filled jars stand shoulder to shoulder across the oilcloth on the table, like fat purple soldiers on parade. Then we escape to the porch, because the steamy kitchen won't be cool until morning.

As I lie in the swaybacked bed, I can hear the chirp of grasshoppers, the wolf singing to its mate, and the owl hooting. The wind rustles the papery corn leaves against one another, and the metal paddles of the windmill clank as they turn slowly. The barn door creaks against its frame, pushed aside by the cat setting out on his nightly hunt. I can't sleep.

Finally, I know what I have to do. I feel the edges of the narrow stairs with my bare toes as I creep softly downstairs. The jars shine purple in the moonlight. I carefully put three of them into Aunt Jane's egg-gathering basket. Before I slip out the screen door, I put in a note for Farmer Wilson that says, *Thank you.*

I sit on the porch steps to put on my shoes so the gravel on the main road won't cut my city-soft feet. It's longer to walk than to ride, but I remember the way. Finally I see the farmer's mailbox. His hound bays lazily in the barn but doesn't come rushing to see who's there. I open the metal front of the box quietly. The jars go into the mailbox, where the farmer will find them tomorrow after the mailman delivers the mail.

I'm still asleep when Aunt Jane climbs the steep stairs to my attic room to wake me. "Must be this clear farm air that makes you sleep so soundly," she says with satisfaction. "Better for you than all that pollution in the city where you live." Downstairs, the eggs on the platter look up at us from their shiny white faces with round yellow eyes.

"Don't you love having me cook breakfast for you?" remarks Aunt Lizzie.

"How did all this dirt get tracked up on the porch?" Aunt Alice wonders aloud.

Later that week, we walk out on the porch. There's a small basket of plums with a note: *Thought you might like some to eat fresh.*

"Now, how did he know it was us?" Aunt Alice wonders. I think to myself that there's no one else in the whole county who drives with her left wheels on the centerline, but I don't say anything.

"You'd probably better take the cane poles and go show him where to find our walleyes," Aunt Alice tells me. "Poor young fellow, can't know anything worth knowing."

I smile to myself.

Finally, at the end of the week, Mom and Dad return. I'm proud to hand them the jar of jam we'll take home.

"Now you'll have something to write about on the first day of school," my mom tells me.

I'll think about my aunts Alice, Lizzie, and Jane eating our jam when the snow swirls, while I'm having some from the jar they gave me.